This book is dedicated to the thousands of Maine children who have completed the Raising Readers program, thereby creating a new generation of readers across the state.

The Libra Foundation, a Maine charitable organization founded by the late Elizabeth Noyce, established Raising Readers in 2000. The goal of Raising Readers is to provide all children in Maine, regardless of their economic means, with a dozen beautiful new books by the time they reach age five. Raising Readers continues to be tremendously successful.

We hope that the children of Maine, armed with a collection of quality Raising Readers books, will continue to pursue lifelong learning by visiting their local libraries and by growing their own personal libraries at home.

To Family Members of Our Five-Year-Old Friend,

Congratulations! You are now the fortunate caretakers of a blossoming five-year-old's mind. We at Raising Readers are thrilled to have been part of your little one's life thus far. Raising Readers, in collaboration with MaineHealth and Eastern Maine Healthcare Systems, has supplied more than one million books to Maine children through their well-child visits since 2000.

We are grateful to all the primary care providers who have partnered with us to deliver a beautiful collection of books to their young patients.

As a five-year-old, your child has just received his or her last book from the Raising Readers program. This book, *Raising Readers: Stories for Maine Children*, written and illustrated by Maine residents, is our special gift to your child. We hope that it will continue to feed that tender flame.

Raising Readers is one of the many organizations that recognize the value of reading to young children. Maine's libraries have offered books and resources to the people of our state for many years. You are probably familiar with your local library. If not, we encourage you and your five-year-old to make a special trip.

During your special visit to the library (whether you are a new or returning member), we invite you to get your five-year-old his or her first library card. Below is a detachable card certifying that your child was "Raised to be a Reader." When you present this card to your library, the librarian will know that your child has a long history of being read to and is eager to borrow books to continue this tradition. Participating libraries will place a special sticker on your child's card that says, "Raising Reader Graduate." This sticker identifies your young reader as part of a group of Maine children who have shared some of the same books at bedtime and storytime during the past five years.

Raising Readers thanks you for the opportunity to pass on our love of children's books and our commitment to early literacy. May your library visits be numerous, and your child's future filled with the joy of reading.

Sincerely,

Lisa Belisle MD
Lisa Belisle, M.D., M.P.H.
Medical Advisor

Diane E. Skog
Diane Skog, M.S.B.
Program Director

Dear Five-Year-Old Friend,

Congratulations! You are a big kid now! Five is a very important birthday. Everything you've learned in the past few years has been preparing you for what is to come. You have many exciting things to look forward to. One of these is reading on your own.

You've probably been reading with those who love you since you were a baby. Reading with other people has helped you to get ready to read by yourself. We hope that some of the reading you've done has been with Raising Readers books.

Raising Readers books are given out by doctors and medical providers who know how important reading is. This is your last Raising Readers book. It is full of stories and pictures created by people from Maine. All of the people who worked to put together this book want you to love reading the way that they do.

We hope you enjoy this book and will keep it for a long time. Some of the stories in it may be easy enough for you to read alone. You may need help for some of the others. The easier ones are in the front of the book, and the harder ones near the back. As you become a better reader, you will be able to read all of the stories by yourself.

Even though this is your last Raising Readers book, your reading adventure is not over. We hope you will continue reading at home and in school. Another great place to explore reading is at your library. Your librarian will be ready to show you a world of wonderful books!

We are so proud of you, our five-year-old friend. May your life be filled with many books, and the joy of reading always.

Sincerely,

Lisa Belisle MD

Lisa M. Belisle, M.D., M.P.H.
Medical Advisor

Diane E. Skog

Diane Skog, M.S.B
Program Director

CONTENTS

Amy MacDonald

Amy MacDonald spent a *lot* of time fixing her kids' bumps, scrapes, and blisters when they were growing up in Falmouth, Maine. Her daughter, Emily, was probably her most frequent Band-Aid customer. So when a friend suggested that she write a poem called "Mr. Fister's Blister," Amy thought the idea had a lot of potential—for a story about a girl!

When Amy was a kid in Beverly, Massachusetts, she read all the time. She had three siblings, and somehow Amy managed to teach herself to read anytime, in any place, no matter how noisy. She even read while she brushed her teeth! Amy visited her local library so regularly that she knew exactly how many steps it was from her front door to the library entrance. She loved books about Nancy Drew and the Hardy Boys, James Bond, and Laura Ingalls Wilder. Other favorites included *Five Children and It* and *The Phoenix and the Carpet* by E. Nesbit, and *The Peterkin Papers* by Lucretia P. Hale.

When Amy wasn't reading or playing on the beach by her house, her favorite place to be was a little cabin at the end of a long dirt road on a pond in the woods of New Hampshire. Her family spent every weekend and most of every summer there. Amy remembers that even though there were no neighbors, no other kids, and no TV or telephone, there was always fun to be had in the woods and on the pond: fishing, swimming, canoeing, sailing, skating.

Amy was in fifth grade when she decided that she wanted to be a writer, and she figured that the best way to learn how to write well was to practice. When she graduated from college, Amy began by working at her local newspaper, the *Harvard Post,* and later by freelancing for magazines. Amy liked newspaper and magazine writing and thought she'd found her career in journalism. But one day she, her husband, and her young son made a trip to visit the cabin in New Hampshire where she had spent so much of her childhood. And on that day, in that place, Amy wrote her first children's book, *Little Beaver and the Echo.* When Amy heard how much people enjoyed her story, she realized she had discovered the kind of writing that she was meant to do.

Another title by Amy MacDonald:

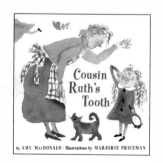

Rachel Fister's Blister

Amy MacDonald

Illustrations by Marjorie Priceman

Houghton Mifflin Company   Boston

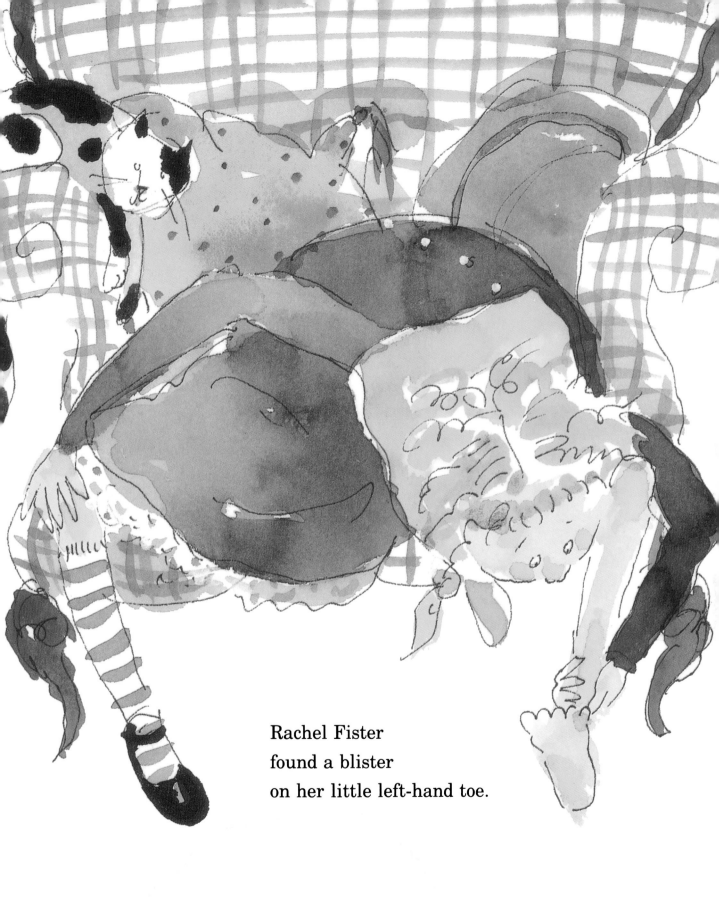

Rachel Fister
found a blister
on her little left-hand toe.

Just a tiny
little blister,
but she thought her mom should know.

Mrs. Fister
saw the blister
on poor Rachel's little toe,

Sent for Mister
(Harvey) Fister,
for she thought he ought to know.

"Don't alarm her.
Bring the farmer!
Call the doctor, call the nurse!

14

"We need help to
fix the blister —
Now — before it gets much worse!

"Find her brothers
and some others.
Send them off to bring some aid.

"Go enlist her
little sister.
Fetch the rabbi. Fetch the maid.

"Quicker! Faster!
Bring the pastor!
Call the postman! Call the priest!

"Faster! Quicker!
Bring the vicar!
Call the fireman! Call the p'lice!

"They'll assist her
with the blister.
Yes, I think they ought to know

"How to fix a
little blister
like the one on Rachel's toe."

21

Pastor Masters
called for plasters —
six or eight or ten or three.

Farmer Chalmer
was much calmer —
he suggested broccoli.

Doctor Proctor
said, "Concoct her
up an herbal remedy,"

24

While the p'liceman
and the postman
both advised a cup of tea.

Rachel's brothers
(and some others)
swore that *ice* would do the trick;

But the fireman
(Roger Byreman)
said that *heat* would cure it quick.

Vicar Wicker
called for liquor
(what he meant was lemonade),

While the maids and
ladies bickered
and the priest and rabbi prayed.

29

Well, they tried them —
they applied them —
one by one to Rachel's toe.

"Darling daughter,
is that better?"
But each time she answered, "No."

"This is irksome.
This is quirksome.
Surely someone ought to know.

"Surely someone
can assist her
with the blister on her toe?"

"Call the palace.
Ask Queen Alice.
She's the smartest,
that's for sure."

So they called her
and appalled her
with their tale of Rachel's cure.

"Fire and ice and
tea and spice!" ex-
claimed the Queen.
"Such silly tips!

"My advice is
quite precise: it's —
listen up! —

35

Just *use your lips*."

"O clever Queen!
(What *can* she mean?)"
Asked the rabbi and the priest.

And the others —
doctors, brothers —
all were stumped, to say the least.

Rachel's mother
said, "Don't bother,
for I think that I can guess."

And she *kissed* her
daughter's blister.
"Is that better, daughter?"

"YES!"

Cathryn Falwell

Although **Cathryn Falwell** considers herself a "Mainer" now, she's actually "from away"—she was born in Kansas City, Kansas, and moved often as a child. By the time she started high school, she had lived in four more states: Missouri, Wisconsin, Minnesota, and Connecticut. Cathryn may have moved around a lot, but her interests in painting, drawing, making things, and reading never changed. When she was in second grade, she announced to her mother that she wanted to make children's books when she grew up . . . and that's exactly what she did!

After studying printmaking at the University of Connecticut, working as a graphic designer and art director, and opening her own graphic design business in Hartford, Cathryn got married, had two sons, and decided that it was time to make her dream of creating children's books come true. Her first book, *Where's Nicky?*, was soon followed by other titles, including *Feast for 10*, *We Have a Baby*, and *Word Wizard*.

Cathryn never lost her love for painting and drawing, but if you look closely at the illustrations in this story, you will discover that a big part of Cathryn's pictures is not paint or pencils but collage! Cathryn loves to mix up all kinds of materials in her illustrations. She uses different kinds of paper, like recycled wrapping paper and grocery bags, and she sometimes will use scraps of cloth, leaf prints, or paint in her illustrations. Cathryn says she tries to think about language in a similar way. Collage is a big part of her writing—she cuts and pastes the best words she can find to tell a story.

A few years after Cathryn started to write and illustrate books, she and her family moved to Frog Song Pond in Gorham, Maine. When she's not working in her studio, Cathryn can be found volunteering, visiting schools, speaking at conferences, leading workshops, and of course drawing, painting, making things, and reading.

Other titles by Cathryn Falwell:

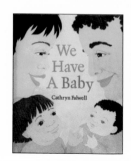
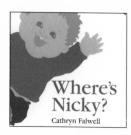

FEAST FOR 10

CATHRYN FALWELL

CLARION BOOKS, NEW YORK

1 one
cart
into the
grocery
store

2 two pumpkins for pie

3 three chickens to fry

4 four children
off to
look for
more

5 five
kinds
of beans

6 six bunches of greens

7

seven
dill pickles
stuffed in
a jar

53

 eight
ripe
tomatoes

9 nine plump potatoes

10 ten
hands
help
to load
the car

Then . . .

1 one
car
home
from the
grocery
store

59

2 two
will
look

3 three will cook

4

four
will
taste
and ask
for
more

5 five empty cans

 **six**
pots and
pans

7 seven
more carrots
to wash
and
peel

8

eight
platters
down

9 nine
chairs
around

10 ten
hungry folks
to share
the
meal!

John and Ann Hassett

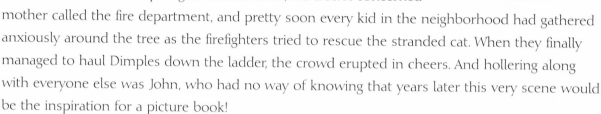

When John Hassett was growing up in Marshfield, Massachusetts, he knew two things about Dimples, the neighborhood cat: Dimples was good at catching mice, and Dimples was bad at climbing trees. John will never forget the summer day when Dimples got stuck in a tall, tall tree. A concerned mother called the fire department, and pretty soon every kid in the neighborhood had gathered anxiously around the tree as the firefighters tried to rescue the stranded cat. When they finally managed to haul Dimples down the ladder, the crowd erupted in cheers. And hollering along with everyone else was John, who had no way of knowing that years later this very scene would be the inspiration for a picture book!

John Hassett has written several stories with his wife, Ann, that include places and people and events that he remembers as a boy. John says their writing is also influenced by his nana, who loved to tell her grandchildren long, wonderfully funny stories.

Quirky humor can be found in a lot of the Hassetts' collaborations. Their other titles include *Charles of the Wild; Father Sun, Mother Moon; The Three Silly Girls Grubb; Mouse in the House; The Finest Christmas Tree;* and, most recently, *Can't Catch Me*. After you read *Cat Up a Tree*, you may want to borrow *Mouse in the House* from the library—Nana Quimby is back for another animal adventure!

Ann and John write and illustrate books in their old yellow farmhouse in Waldoboro, on the east coast of Maine, and animals are a big part of their lives. Over the years, their house and barn have been home to a cow, four sheep, a guinea pig, a white rabbit, two dogs, a cat, twenty-three chickens, three goats, and mice in the walls. In addition to animals and their two daughters, they are surrounded by trees, fields, saltwater coves, and other children's book authors, who John says are as common to Maine as pine cones in the forest.

Other titles by John and Ann Hassett:

Cat Up a Tree

John and Ann Hassett

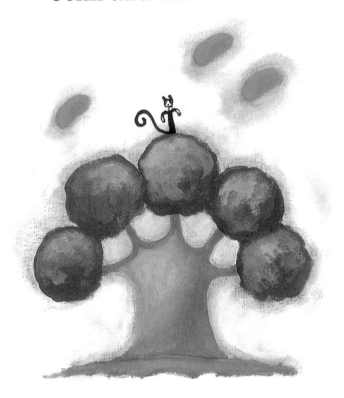

HOUGHTON MIFFLIN COMPANY BOSTON

Walter Lorraine Books

Nana Quimby went to the window
and saw a cat up a tree.
She rang the firehouse on her telephone.
"Help!" she cried. "Cat up a tree."

"Sorry," said the firehouse, "we do not catch cats up a tree anymore. Call back if that cat starts playing with matches."

Nana Quimby went to the window and counted five cats up the tree. She rang the police station.

"Help!" she cried. "Five cats up a tree."

"Sorry," said the police station, "we do not catch cats up a tree. Call back if the cats rob a bank."

Nana Quimby went to the window and
counted ten cats up the tree.
She rang the pet shop. "Help!" she cried.
"Ten cats up a tree."

"Sorry," said the pet shop,
"we do not catch cats up a tree.
Call back if the cats wish to buy a dog."

Nana Quimby went to the window and
counted fifteen cats up the tree.
She rang the zoo. "Help!" she cried.
"Fifteen cats up a tree."

"Sorry," said the zoo,
"we do not catch cats up a tree.
Call back if one of the cats is tall and
has stripes—our tiger is missing."

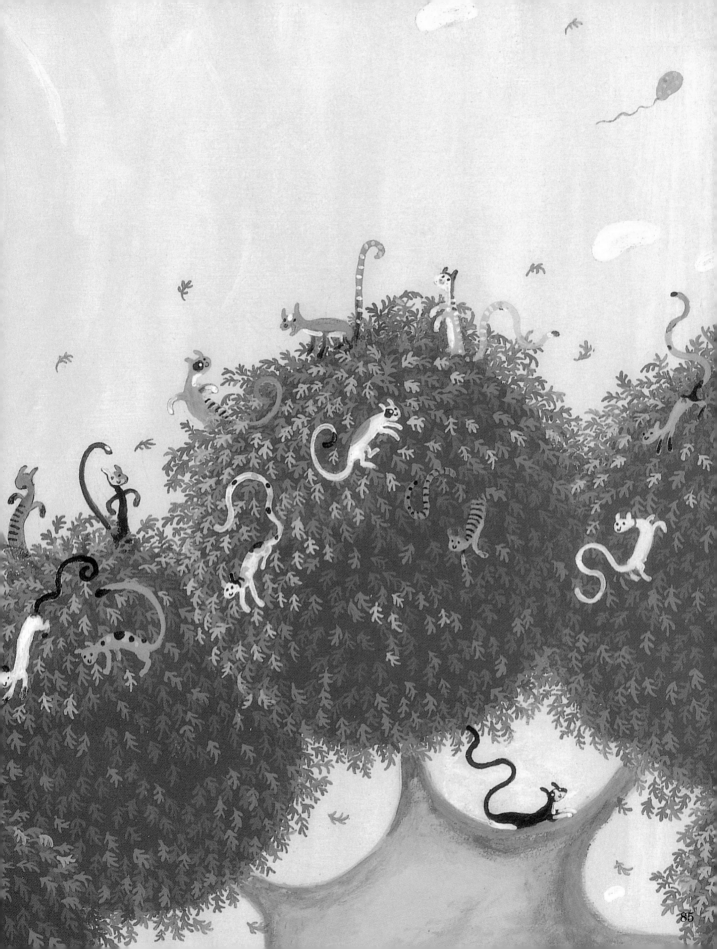

Nana Quimby went to the
window and counted twenty
cats up the tree.
She rang the post office.
"Help!" she cried.
"Twenty cats up a tree."

"Sorry," said the post office,
"we do not catch cats up a
tree. Call back if the cats
are sending a postcard and
need stamps."

Nana Quimby went to
the window and counted
twenty-five cats up the tree.
She rang the library.
"Help!" she cried.
"Twenty-five cats up a tree."

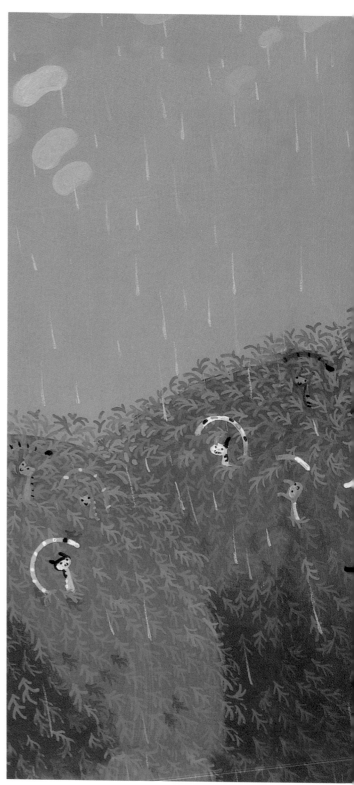

"Sorry," said the library,
"we do not catch cats up
a tree. Call back if the cats
have an overdue book."

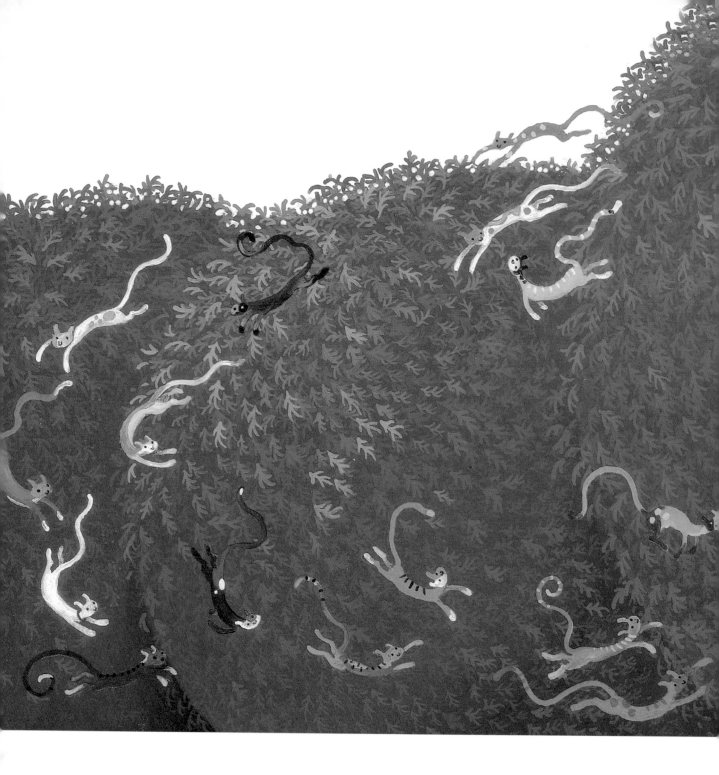

Nana Quimby went to the window

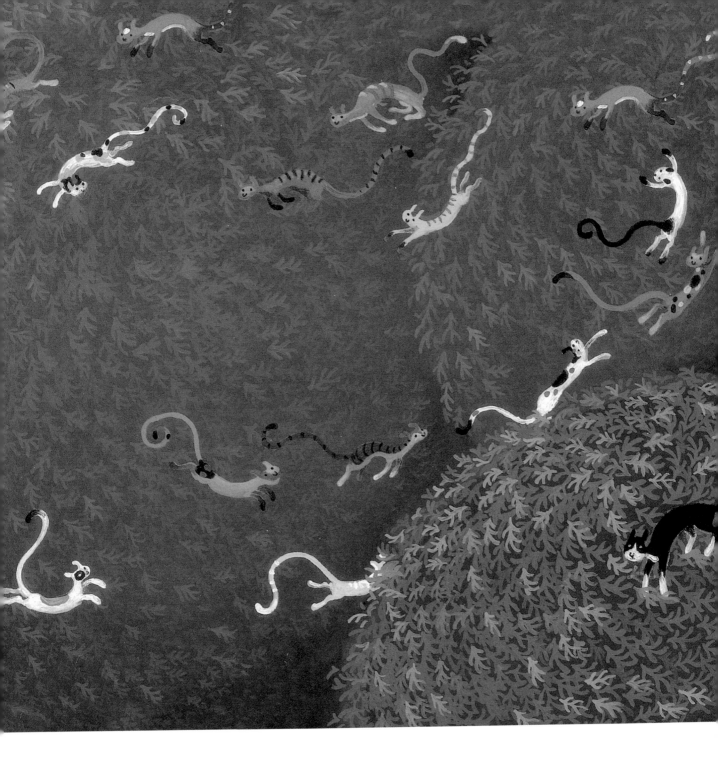

and counted thirty cats up the tree.

She rang city hall. "Help!" she cried. "Thirty cats up a tree."

"Sorry," said city hall, "we do not catch cats up a tree.
Call back if you need a sign that says Danger! Look up for
Falling Cats."

So when Nana Quimby went to the window and counted

thirty-five cats up the tree, she threw the telephone out the window.

Then forty cats tiptoed across the telephone line

and hopped in the window into Nana Quimby's arms.

Later, Nana Quimby's telephone rang—it was city hall!

"*Help!*" cried city hall.
"*Mice in the firehouse,
mice in the jail,
mice in books,
mice in the mail.
Mouse here,
mouse there—
millions of mouses
EVERYWHERE!*"

"Sorry," said Nana Quimby, "the cats do not catch mice anymore. Call back if you wish to hear cats *purr.*" She set the phone down softly, for too many cats to count were having a nap.

Lisa Jahn-Clough

Until she was ten years old, Lisa Jahn-Clough lived on a small Rhode Island farm where she had a best friend, an older brother, and Mother Nature as playmates. With acres of woods to explore and the ocean at the end of the road, Lisa was familiar with all sorts of land and sea creatures—even the ones that weren't native to New England. Lisa's dad was a zoologist, and what Lisa couldn't find outside, she sometimes discovered in her own home!

Lisa wrote lots of stories when she was young. She wrote books before she even learned how to write. When Lisa had a story idea in mind, she told it aloud it to her father and he wrote her words down in a little book of blank pages tied together with string. Once the story was written, Lisa illustrated it. She still has her very first homemade book, called "The Little Girl."

When Lisa wasn't writing about girls, she was reading about them. Characters like Eloise, Ramona, Harriet the Spy, Mary from *The Secret Garden*, the March girls from *Little Women*, and true stories about real scientists, writers, astrologers, and pioneer women fascinated her. She also spent a lot of time painting, drawing, and cutting and pasting.

Both people and animals have inspired Lisa to write and illustrate all kinds of stories, which include *On the Hill, Alicia Has a Bad Day, Simon and Molly Plus Hester*, and of course *Little Dog*. Lisa doesn't need to look farther than her own backyard to remember what inspired her to write *Little Dog*. A few years ago, Lisa adopted a stray dog named Happy, and her life hasn't been the same since. Dog love, says Lisa, is pure joy, and Happy has enriched her life in ways that she never thought possible.

When Lisa was growing up, her family spent almost every summer on Monhegan Island, off the Maine coast. So when they eventually moved to Portland, she already felt a strong connection to the state. Today, Lisa still makes her home in Portland, where she has taught people about writing and illustrating for many years . . . and of course she's been doing some writing and illustrating herself!

Other titles by Lisa Jahn-Clough:

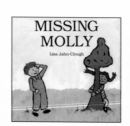

LITTLE DOG

by Lisa Jahn-Clough

Houghton Mifflin Company Boston 2006

Walter Lorraine Books

Little Dog lived on the streets.

Little Dog was hungry. He was tired.
He wanted to eat and sleep and chase things.

Most of all, he wanted someone to love.

Little Dog roamed the city.
Everyone told him to scram.

It was a hard life, but
Little Dog kept hoping.

One day there was a big festival.
No one noticed Little Dog.

Little Dog slipped into a building.
In the back someone was hanging a painting.

Rosa was an artist.

Her paintings were sad and dark.

Little Dog took a chance and rolled on Rosa's feet.

"A little dog!" Rosa said. "Want some food?"
Little Dog's tail went thump, thump, thump.

"You're so scruffy. You're so scrappy,"
Rosa said. "But you're so happy."
Little Dog's tail thumped faster.
"You can stay," said Rosa.

Rosa gave Little Dog a sudsy bath and
made him a cozy place to sleep.

In the morning Rosa and Little Dog went out.

Rosa started to paint with her usual dark colors.

Little Dog pranced around.

"This doesn't feel right," Rosa said.

"I don't want to paint these
gloomy pictures anymore."
Little Dog wriggled with joy.

"What can I do?" cried Rosa.

Little Dog woofed and yipped and wagged his tail.

"Where are you going, Little Dog? Wait for me!"

Rosa followed Little Dog a long way.
The city buildings changed to houses
and then to hills with trees and flowers.

They were in the country!

Little Dog took a deep breath.
The air smelled of fresh grass and
lots of creatures to chase.

124

Rosa took out her paints.
The world was full of color
and growing things.

125

Little Dog frolicked and Rosa painted.
When the sun began to set they packed up.
"What a beautiful day this has been," Rosa said.
Little Dog yipped in delight.

When they got back to the city
everything looked different.
Little Dog played while Rosa
painted and painted and painted.

Finally Rosa hung up her new paintings.

Everyone admired Rosa's art.
"So bright! So cheerful!" they said.

"Thank you," Rosa said.

"I could not have done it without Little Dog."

Little Dog looked at the paintings.
He was in every one.

Little Dog jumped into Rosa's arms.
"I'm so happy you found me," said Rosa.
Little Dog was happy, too.

Epilogue

Rosa and Little Dog moved to the country.
Rosa had plenty of colorful things to paint.
Little Dog had plenty of food to eat, time to nap,
creatures to chase, and lots of love.

Melissa Sweet

Melissa Sweet's third grade teacher, Mrs. Blockburger, called Melissa her "wee lass." But Mrs. Blockburger knew as well as anyone else who saw Melissa's artwork that Melissa was hugely talented.

Melissa always thought she'd be an artist. When she got to high school she tried pottery, but when she went to art school she fell in love with painting and drawing. When Melissa rediscovered Maurice Sendak's *Little Bear*, she decided that book illustration and her artistic style might go hand in hand.

Other people agreed. After putting together a collection of her own greeting cards and handmade books, Melissa went to New York to show her work to art directors in the city. She came back with her very first assignment: to illustrate the Pinky and Rex series by James Howe. Melissa remembers how incredibly thrilling it was to illustrate her first books. She's illustrated more than sixty books since, including *The Boy Who Drew Birds* by Jacqueline Davies and *Chicken Joy on Redbean Road* by Jacqueline Briggs Martin, and she's still excited!

Carmine: A Little More Red is the very first book that Melissa both wrote and illustrated. When she looks back on her childhood in northern New Jersey, she remembers spending a *lot* of time on her bicycle—just like Carmine. But instead of riding her bike to Granny's house for alphabet soup, Melissa would pay a visit to Percy's store for penny candy and comic books and then play with the other kids in the neighborhood until the fireflies twinkled and their parents called them in to bed.

Melissa came to Maine as an adult and now lives in Rockport with her husband, her stepdaughter, and her trusty dogs, Rufus and Nellie.

Other titles illustrated by Melissa Sweet:

   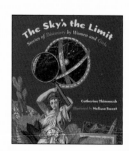

Carmine
A Little More Red

By Melissa Sweet

Houghton Mifflin Company
Boston 2005

Granny's house

to the
Wolf's den

Carmine's house

ABECEDARIAN: ALPHABETICALLY ARRANGED

alphabet

Carmine had a beloved granny who taught her how to read by making ALPHABET soup. Granny spooned the letters to form a word and before long Carmine was reading the whole bowl. Whenever Granny makes a pot of alphabet soup she invites Carmine to lunch.

beware

On this day, as always, Granny told Carmine it was important to stay on the path and BEWARE of dangers along the way.

clutter

Carmine rummaged through her CLUTTER and gathered up pencils, paper, and paint, and anything else she might need along the way to Granny's.

dilly-dally

Some people DILLY-DALLY once in a while, but Carmine made a habit of it. Carmine's mother reminded her to go directly there, please. No dawdling.

Don't dilly-dally—your granny will be waiting.

'Bye!

Okay 'Bye!

Carmine and Rufus took off through the woods. They rode up
and down the hillsides until they came to the edge of a field.
There were some big tracks along the path. Rufus kept sniffing the
air. Still, Carmine thought this looked like a safe enough place—just to
stop and rest.

exquisite

It was a clear morning. The light was EXQUISITE. Carmine began making a picture for Granny.

farther

She started filling her painting with color. It may seem farfetched to think that any painting can be improved by adding a little more red, but Carmine believes it to be true. The poppies in the distance caught her eye, and she wandered FARTHER to get a better look.

green

Walking along, carrying her easel, Carmine noticed how the sunlight flickered on the tall GREEN grass, the ferns and flowers. She made sketches in her notebook. Granny would love this painting best of all.

seed pod

Papaver rhoeas

haiku

Thinking of Granny, Carmine wrote a HAIKU:

My Granny is plump.
Her soup will make you want more
The secret is bones.

indeed

Meanwhile, Rufus noticed an odd scent in the air. INDEED, he knew a wolf when he smelled one.

joke

Rufus was nervous at the thought of a wolf nearby. It is no JOKE that a wolf could eat a dog in the blink of an eye.

knoll

By now Carmine was far away on a **KNOLL**. She could see Granny's house and even Granny's sheep way in the distance. And she could still see Rufus, but just barely.

lurking

Most wolves practice the fine art of LURKING.

mimic

A mockingbird landed above Carmine's head. Mockingbirds are famous for their ability to MIMIC sounds of all kinds; this one was snarling and growling and licking its chops. It even howled.

nincompoop

Everyone knows it isn't very nice to call a person, or even a bird, a
NINCOMPOOP, but sometimes Carmine could not help herself.

omen

The mockingbird reminded Carmine that her granny had heard a wolf howl just last night. She wondered if this bird was a sign of trouble—a bad OMEN.

pluck

Anyone else might have gotten the heebie-jeebies from a bird making sounds like that. But Carmine had a good deal of PLUCK. She rolled up her sleeves and went back to painting.

quiver

A rustling noise in the bushes made Rufus QUIVER.

reckoned

Rufus RECKONED this was a full-fledged wolf in front of him. He could tell by the large eyes, big ears, and long nose and teeth.

surreal

Rufus began to bark, and the wolf knew exactly what he was saying. SURREAL as it may seem, dogs are descendants of wolves, and it made sense that the wolf could understand his language.

It took the wolf just a little while to get to Granny's house.

trouble

As soon as Granny spotted the wolf outside, she grabbed the key to lock the door—she didn't want any TROUBLE— but it was too late.

Granny screamed at the top of her lungs. Doors slammed and pots clattered. Granny saw her kitchen turned upside down. Then it went quiet.

usually

USUALLY the neighbors are home and would have heard Granny's cry for help. And usually a woodcutter is around, but on this day he was deep in the woods, felling trees for a treehouse.

voilà*

"**VOILÀ!**" Carmine had just exclaimed as she finished her painting.
It was at that moment she heard the cry—"WOLF!"

*It means "there you are, there you have it" (in French).

161

worry

When she heard the cry, she was filled with WORRY.
Carmine raced to Granny's as fast as she could.

x-ray

No one really has X-RAY vision except superheroes. Carmine was not a superhero. At the little white house, all she could see of Granny were her glasses flung across the floor. There were tracks and footprints, but no Granny.

Meanwhile, back at his den, the wolf held out an armful of bones.
His pups began to yap their heads off.

yodel

When all hope seemed lost, Carmine and Rufus heard an odd noise—sort of like a YODEL. The sound made Rufus berserk. Carmine yanked on the closet door.

One day you head out down the road with no worries. The next moment, you think your granny has been eaten up by a wolf. But just as quickly—voilà!—here she is, hiding in a closet, yodeling. And everything is okay again. It's zany.

zillion

Granny and Carmine served up the alphabet soup. Rufus ate a bone the wolf left behind. Granny reminded Carmine that she had been told a **ZILLION** times not to dilly-dally in the woods. Carmine said that she would never dawdle again. She gave her granny the painting she had done, and Granny hung it on the wall with the rest of Carmine's pictures.

Carmine and Rufus zoomed home. They didn't stop once.

169

DEDICATIONS

Rachel Fister's Blister
For Emily – A.M.
For Elizabeth – M.P.

Feast for 10
For my family
in loving memory of my grandmothers,
Willie Mae McMullen Chauvin and Evelyn Haning Falwell,
who often made feasts for plenty

Cat Up a Tree
For Michael, David, Ryan, Torrie, Jackie, Bobby, and Lauren

Little Dog
For Happy
Thanks to Mom

Carmine: A Little More Red
To Mark and Emily.
And to my editor, Ann Rider—a ZILLION thanks.

CATHRYN · FALWELL

FEAST FOR 10

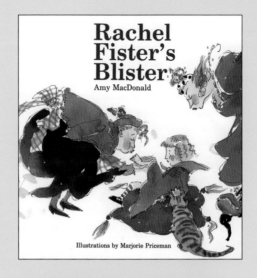

Rachel
Fister's
Blister

Amy MacDonald

Illustrations by Marjorie Priceman

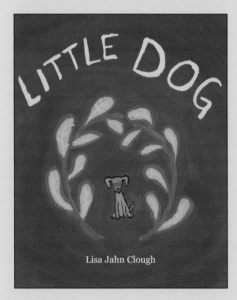

LITTLE DOG

Lisa Jahn Clough

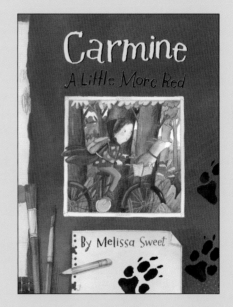

Carmine
A Little More Red

By Melissa Sweet

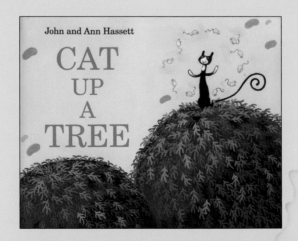

John and Ann Hassett

CAT
UP
A
TREE